# How the Muse Plays His Lyre

SEBASTIAN BERNINZONI

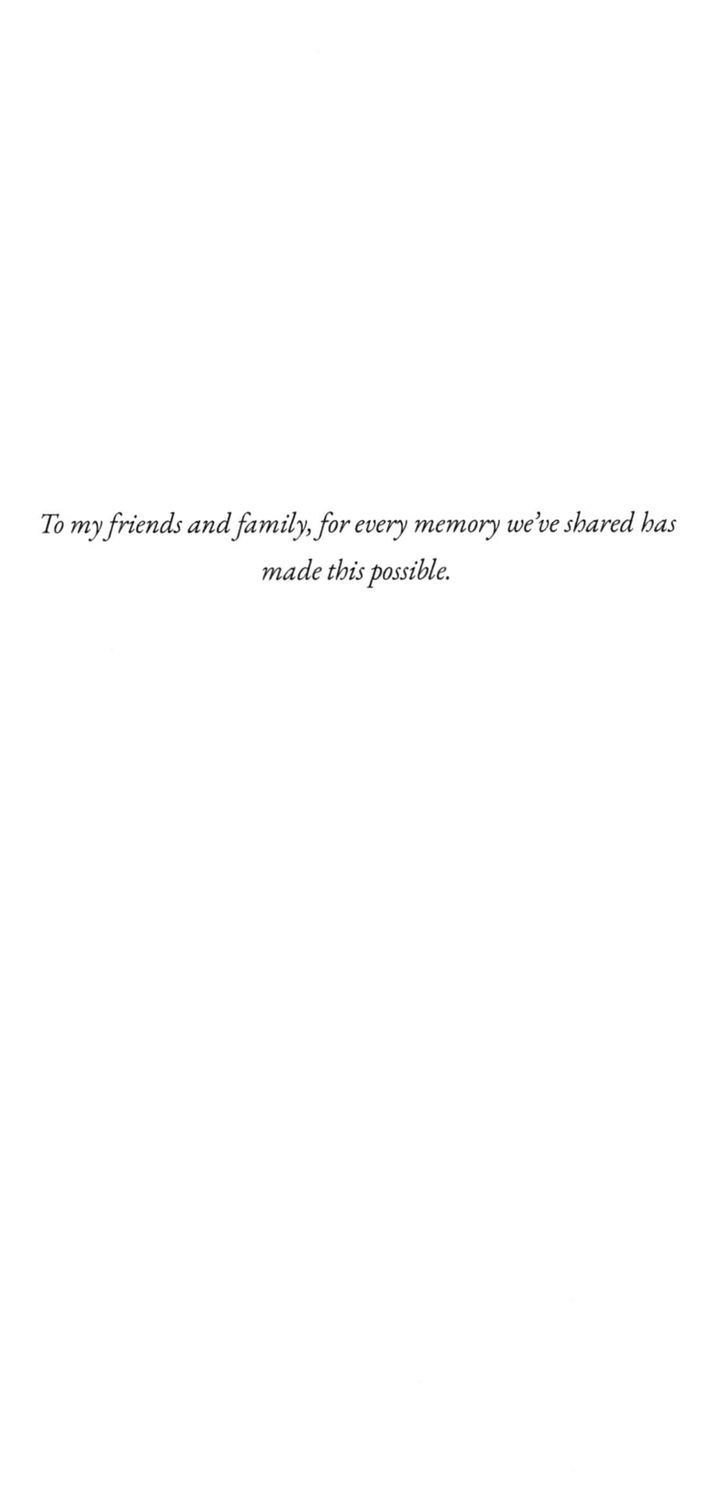

*To my friends and family, for every memory we've shared has made this possible.*

There is nothing permanent except change.

—Heraclitus

# ACT I
## PROTASIS

When I went back home and pulled up in my four-door car,
you put holiday decorations on your glass door
for the fawn hiding off the road.


Kind of like a never-changing happy ending.
It made me love every word and thing you gave me—
and syllable
and letter.
I held them between my two front teeth,
while fate whispered it would never work out.


Before I tell you *how*, I feel that I should tell you *why*.
We did everything together. We even started to smell the same—like old books and white clay.
Being with you was like the protection of a coffin.
I was no longer afraid of the kids stomping along our grave once I realized you made me a fool.
I knew I was alive! I didn't want some premature burial just to make you happy.


You told me you're moving to Boston. I forced a smile in your direction and listened to your misguided, shiny objectives.
I'm sick of hearing about cherry-flavored vodka and the bowling pins of your friends.
I told you that things had to change—for better or for worse. I mean, you were the one who told me that "there's no place like New York City."

Right?

The motive of this murder of us was that I simply needed to protect something in myself.

So, that night, I decided to cut you off.

Just like that.

But fate also destined me for the longing of your hand.

I think we sat at breakfast, over millennialized food and drink, the next morning.

Silence was a tangible thing back then. I wish I knew what it looked like so I could tell you, but I knew it was there:

the room, full when empty, yet so empty when full.

Vacant tables meant the silence had to go somewhere. It could have gone out of the swinging screen doors, but I think it preferred to stand in our dissonance.

Cruel.

Cruel little thing fate is.

For no one's ever loved me like you have

and no one ever will

and no one's ever gonna know that, for some odd reason, I've never loved you more than I do right now.

I still expect letters from you, even though that perception of your character never even existed. There is a kind of electric white that I think of when I think of you.

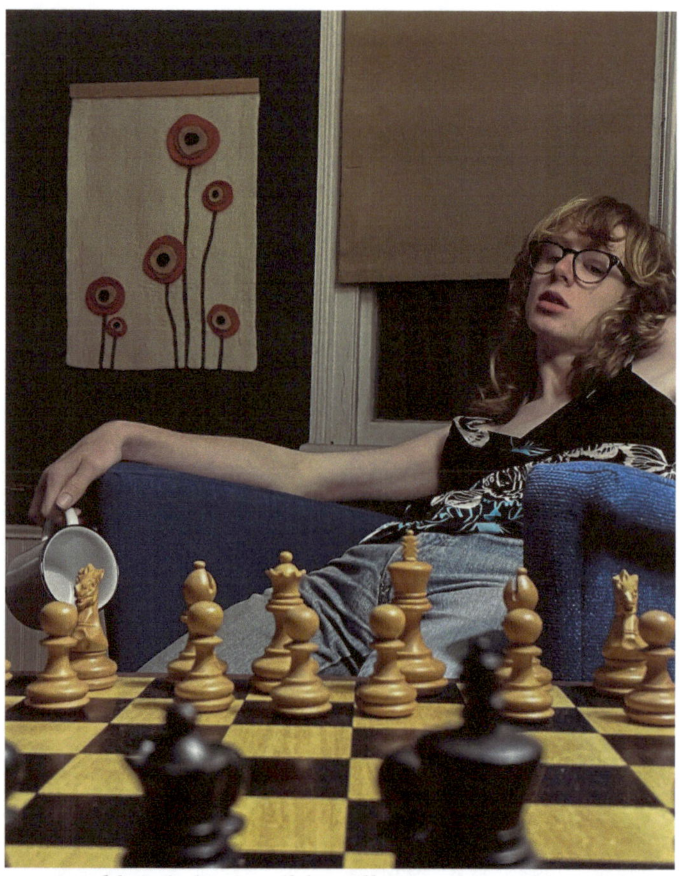

*I couldn't shake you off, but I'll write about it like I did.*


The tip of my ballpoint pen says:


*Fuck us.*


And fuck your shitty parking job.

From my shoulder to yours, because my throat hurts when you're the one it's calling. It's me and you and our simple summer, where at the sink we stood with nothing said but an early morning nod.

I swear you would stare at me so intently back then, as if the first person to stop brushing their teeth would lose this imaginary contest.

At the three-minute mark, it got intense.

Toothpaste foam flooded from the corners of your mouth, and I kind of tilted my head to get a closer look. I think I remember wanting to lick it from your face.

Not lustfully, but in a more nurturing way—unlike so many of your Brooklyn hookups.

To this day, I still talk about your stupid kids' toothpaste, and I hate how I actually prefer it to mine. Maybe it reminds me of you.

Or your mouth.

Or maybe it's just damn good.

You changed and challenged me like that, questioning what maturity really means—if I really like boring Colgate at the crack of dawn.

The end of our sabbatical led to hollower hallways and clearer clicks of shined shoes on linoleum floors. You would have called me lonely, but I haven't shed a single tear.

When I stay up at night and stare at the wall at the foot of my bed, I no longer imagine my head in your lap. Instead, I watch the occasional reflection of headlights pass through my eastern-facing window.

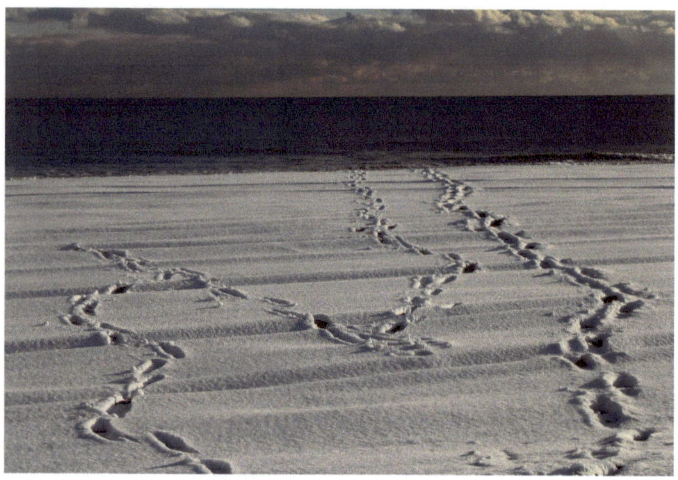

*"Let's go our separate ways."*

Your palms sounded like birds chirping in the seemingly dark chasm of your heart.

It should have been warm.

Hot, even.

But your palms were the warmest thing I held in sight on some random August night.

Who was I to say no? Or resist?


I knew you knew the true nature of my fear.

The fear of a stab-and-twist, left to bleed.

Not a fear of the dark.

Because I'm not a fucking child after all.

Because I'm fifteen going on fifty-one.

I think. I mean, that's what everyone's been telling me since I opened my eyes.


What God knows is that I kept the love note I wrote for you in my wallet for way too long, yet it fell just short of your desires.

You read it with a nonchalant adolescence that only I would excuse as apathy.

I run a boiling shower while weighing the possibilities.

It could be soap in my eyes or mouth, but hopefully it lathers just right.


The note has found its way back to me as I returned.

Lights off,

in the dark,

with complete silence.

Quickly tainted by my sinless hair,
dripping down onto the page,
making the lines of the loose-leaf paper bleed in cold murder.
Blue antifreeze against my firefly lightning.

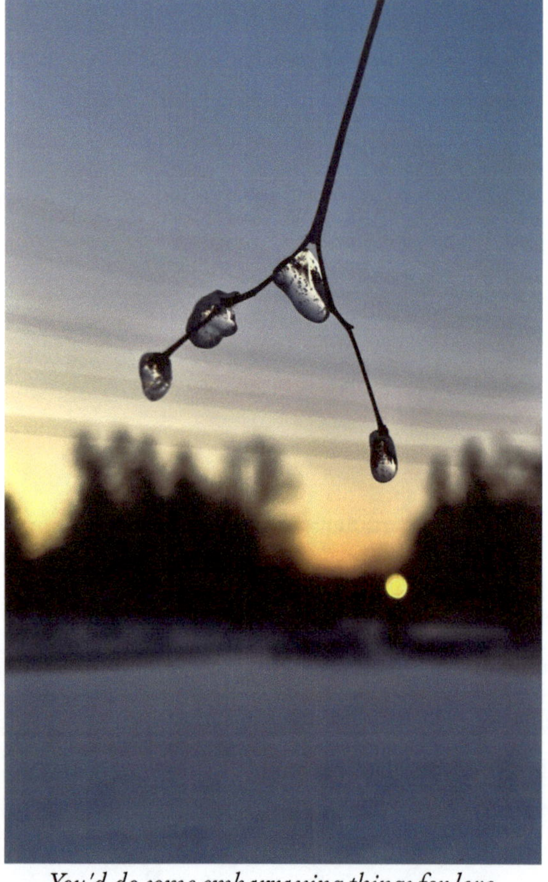

*You'd do some embarrassing things for love.*

WHY *US* WAS CLANDESTINE:

- Your warm palms.

- Your shitty handwriting.

- Your deep voice but young cadence.

- Your beach-blond hair that smells like Old Spice.

- Your flaunting of baggy streetwear (deemed by god to be apathy).

- People dying.

- Our kissing (of others).

- That's all.




- I thought I could change your mind.

*Example one*

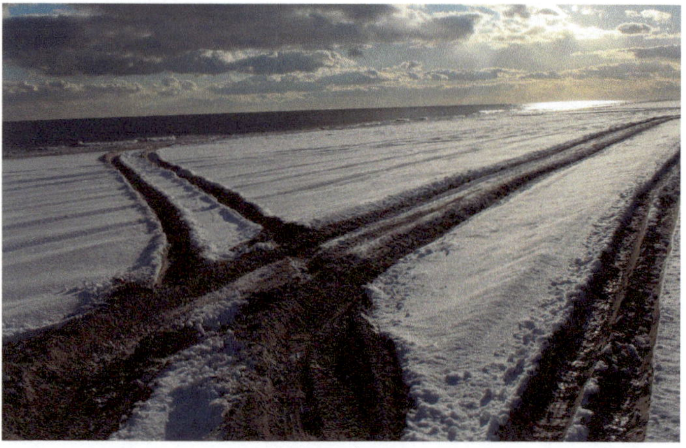

*Example two*

Eclipsed by the chilled glass,

flourishing and fluorescent over-fertilized leaves.

Stark yellow-stained windows—like those of cathedrals—cast this rich butter light on partly cloudy afternoons.

I look away for too long, and just like that—it's night.

Oncoming headlights catch on your stubble—or peach fuzz (no one is too sure about your face like that).


Staring at your face, I'm reminded of some antithetical, begrudging family vacations:

The heavy colonial bell that resides in a shell of our meeting place under cloud cover, and the pedal on my bike.

They all bring me home to that typewriter, desk, and necklace.

This time, the antiquated clicks are ridden with a pleasant, sickening lavender.

Because "where the music ends, the cicadas start."

Perfect. Too perfect.

You're not listening. It's too with two O's like "too" not "to" or "two" or "three."


In the end, though, I know what I want.

It's a shield for us.

From some kind of bigotry—

any kind of bigotry.

And maybe next on my list would be World Peace

and a caption below:

"Disillusionment."

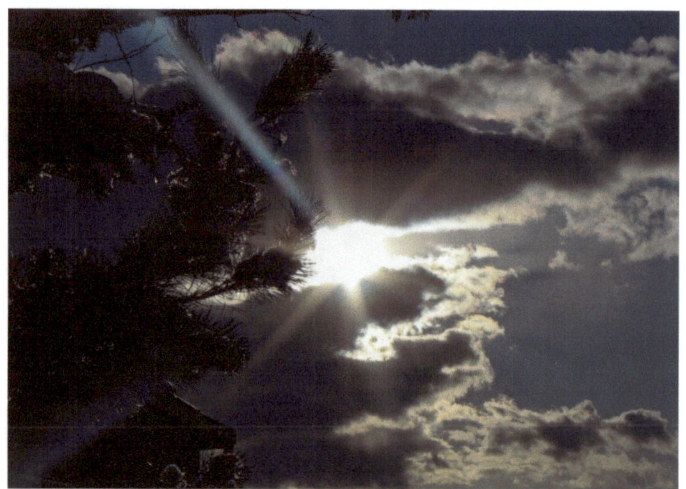

*Vacation homes.*

Anyways, I'm getting dropped off by this driver of mine, whereas we used to take these state-of-the-art trains.

Did you know where they could take us?

Anywhere.

Anywhere you wanted.

From that tiny vision of the big world that you have.

So big, in fact, that CNN's humanitarian crises only hurt our American ears—not leave them bloodied and stained with death.

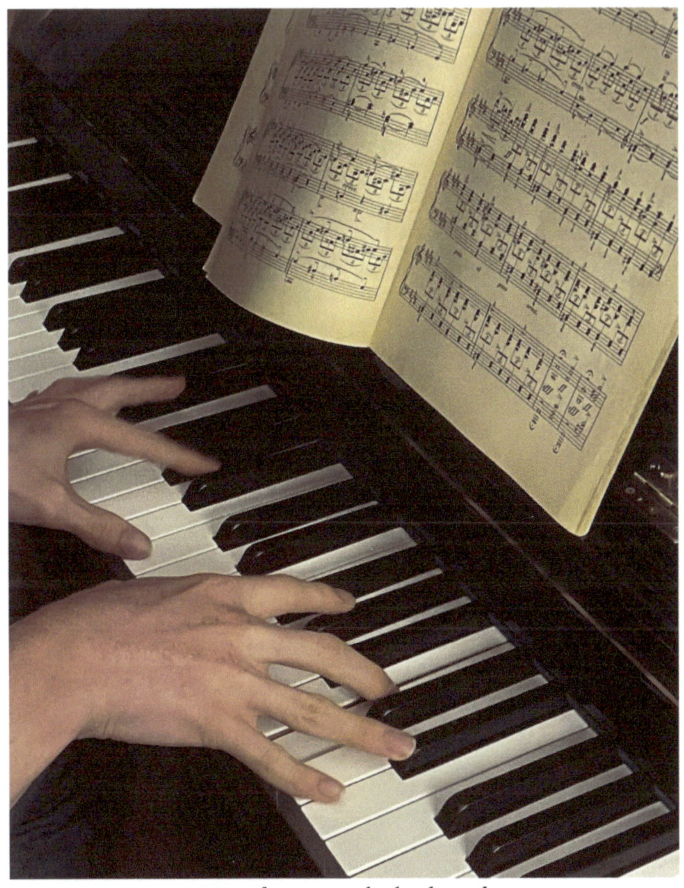

*38 miles across the keyboard.*

# ACT II

## EPITASIS

I used to be a boy who would go on fishing trips.

Cedar planks gave me splinters,

and I could only remove them when I got home.

My hair fell differently.

A new curl pattern and the faded scar on my forehead tell me

what's different from then to now.

I wore strange hats and horrible jokes on my head and my

sleeves.

It's just like knowing too much but yet nothing at all.


When did I become complex or interesting enough to talk to?

When did I become enough?

And was it the same time I sat down and got boring?


I got my learner's permit.

So, some time between your cry and my drive, I learned the

distinction between August and November,

and Massachusetts and Tennessee.


Everything between my nail-bed and the dirt happened at six.

Where, for a minute, I might have been the son you wanted—

playing football in the yard at nine

and learning to golf at twelve.

So I wanted to tell you that I never hated going fishing—

turning an animal into food.

From a verb to a noun.

And now I guess I get my beauty sleep

     SEBASTIAN BERNINZONI

in a bed with no friends or top sheet.

I'll frequently continue to slip on my dreams
and ask what they mean
in a room full of psychologists and analysts.
The only thing I can think of is:
Who am I to remember this?

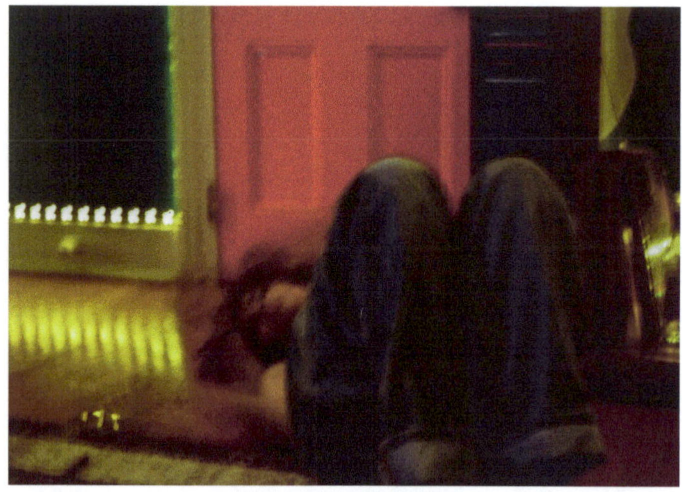

*Boy v. Olympic Games*

*IT'S BEAUTIFUL ISN'T IT?*

Startled, I strangled my gaze from my antiquated home-video camera's viewfinder to find a fifth-floor priestess.

Matte bomber-jacket vinyl diffusing the white street light.

My lips fell into my mouth as a nervous habit. To some degree, chapped winter lips feel comforting.

MHM.

Said tentatively.

*WHATCHU TAKING PICTURES OF THE MOON FOR?*

A school assignment.

I'M NOT SURE.

At the street corner, it was more than just a picture.

*IT'S NOT EVEN A FULL MOON.*

What a way to crush a child's spirit.

SO?

She patted me on the shoulder and left to stand in the lobby-light and art-deco-powered baseboard heating.

I suppose I've been searching for that patronizing answer this whole time.

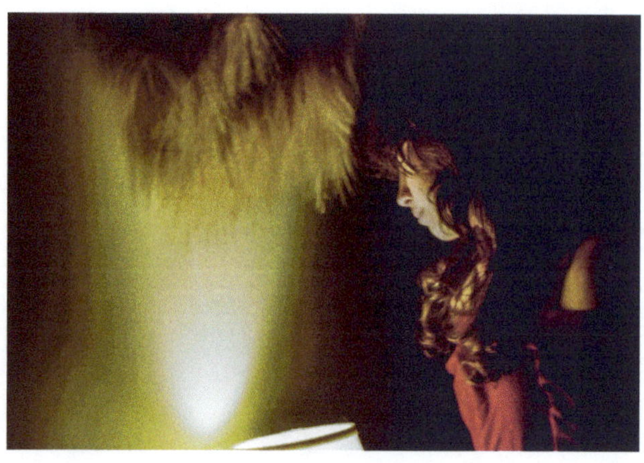

SUBURBAN EXTERMINATION:

- Self-loathing

- Ancient literature

- Radical hatred

- Crossed-out (Grey) dreams

- New snow covenant

- The media

- And anagrams

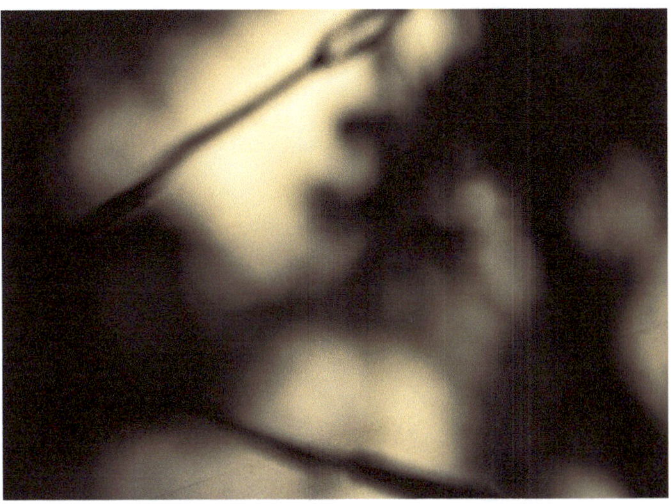

*Twelve years of english class and counting.*

The answer.

It came to me in a dream.

She called it "J-Word Friends"

I thought she wrote it about me.

Spinal cord straight. Ironed out and sobered up.

Now I stare into mirrors that I thought were my friends

and I squint

really, really hard,

just trying to get a glimpse of her.


I've started to see what she means.

Every vein in my body was frozen as I moved towards lace.

Perfect. Made to cover something up. Something human.
Something raw. Something I would never say.

Like how in Great Neck her brother drives way too fast, and
their proximity to the Queensboro bridge is almost sickening.

I keep going back to the question of how our lives compare.
For some reason I think of a thousand paper hearts, made from
recycled, Christmas tissue paper.

If you ignore the agonizing traffic, Westchester is really only
around forty-five minutes away.

Where the birthday girl is screaming upstairs.

Filthy Nikes and the baggiest jeans sweeping the floor.

Bottles on bottles and random excited shouts that would
normally bother me,

but instead, I laid my head back on the browned antique
couch,

the kind that sinks inches from the floor when you sit on it,

while lithe figures of my friends danced around like drunken, foreign angels.

The music winding down and the vinyl crackling, symbolizing nothing other than the start of the evening.

We all stumble outside together onto the front porch with peeling red paint.

The all-consuming stars are louder than the over-packed Q train.

Among the vastness of the universe above me, I think about others who live and breathe only one, ever-changing thing, constantly moving away from the "simple pleasures" I described in that argumentative essay last year.

I began to choke on the thick, hedonistic smoke that dripped out of these hysterical strangers' mouths.


Since then, I've been sitting at the bottom of this misused martini glass— empty and spent with some kind of inertia.

My sweat sticks to my skin like the dregs at the bottom of an almost empty bottle of 110 proof liquor.

I'm searching for a reference, or some kind of "inner-guide".

I try to forcefully recall the strumming of the guitar, feet on the "dash", or a peaceful meditation surrounded by beds of soft pine needles.

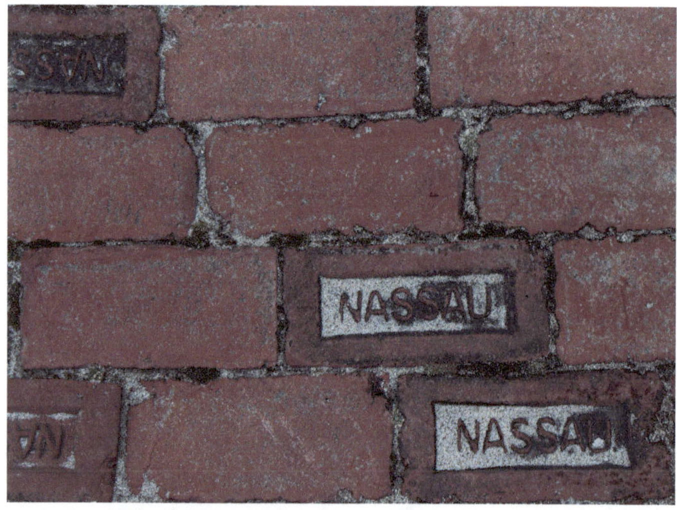


*Take the Long Island Expressway, Eastbound.*

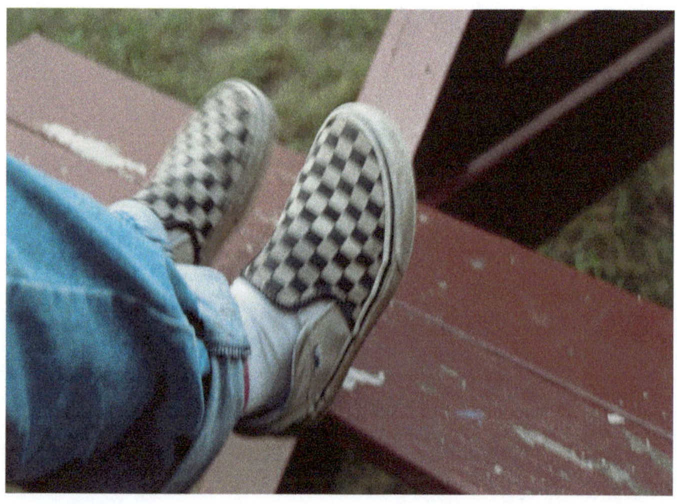

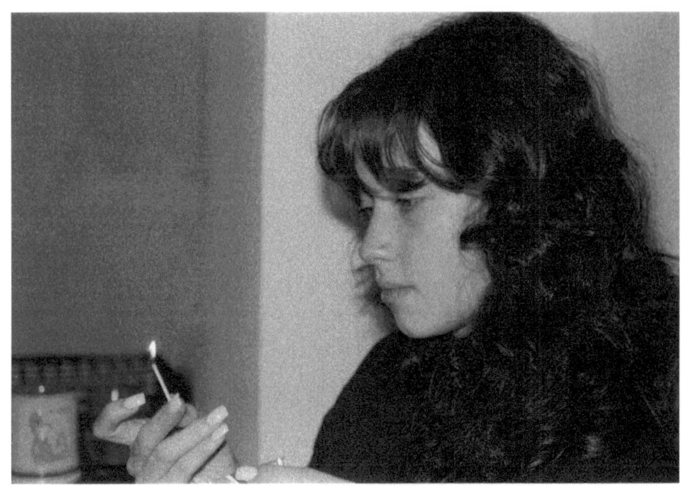

*It's all one big joke.*

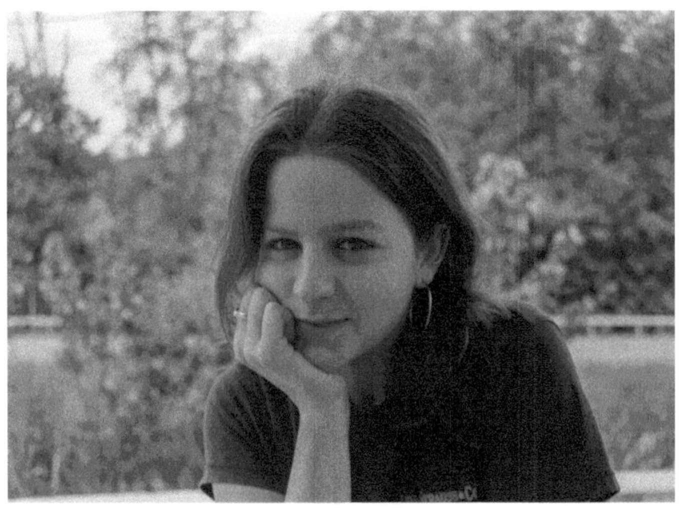

My irreverence is becoming more and more difficult.

The apathy picket fence has a toll booth, and it averages around the price of gasoline.

War, pain, suffering: all good reasons for my "grounding."

When it comes crashing down, do I have time to move to the sidelines?

Do I have time to turn eighteen? To make my pick and get a sticker?

Typical how my alliteration falls apart once I get to the good stuff.

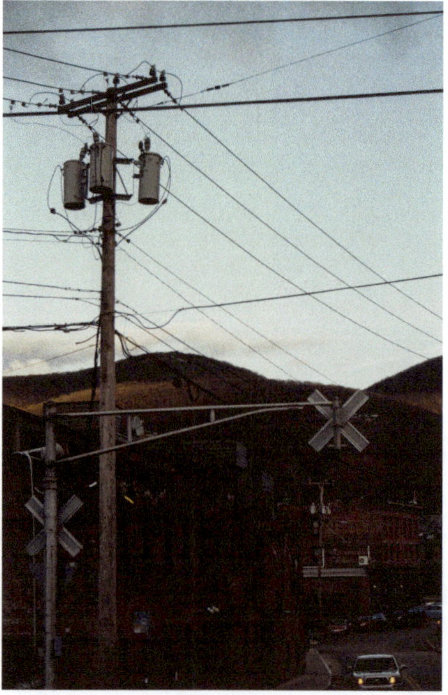

*I voted!*

## PROTECT CHILDREN FROM DRAG QUEENS

Who would've thought—

that gay kid gots feelings.

Feelings that you don't like him.

How, when he comes around, things get real quiet.

How he doesn't use the school bathroom and no one understands why.

Even when the carvings in the stall's walls describe all of his shortfalls.

He's even more afraid now.

He learned the word *faggot* before the word *gay*.

Do you know how kids learn a 6-letter word before a 3-letter one?

It's too late now. They're already inscribed on the insides of his eyes.

He's fucked up. One can only abet in his indisposition now, afflicted by maladies.

Knives that would gut either side of his larynx.

God forbid he move.

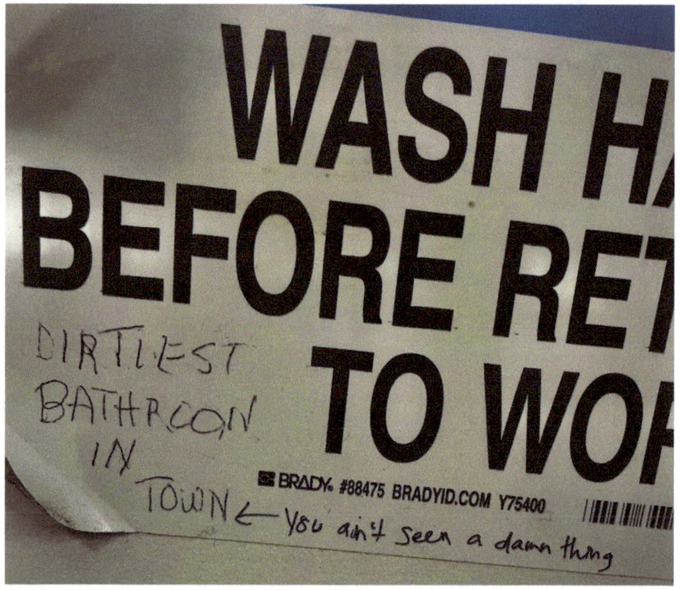


*How is it you tell him that he isn't enough, but too much at the
same time?*

Feel that pity? After that last poem, you must.

Yet, I wish I could play off my life like some kind of Greek
drama.

Yet, I keep grieving and can't stop.

Grief of loathing, bubble-baths to billboard forecasts came
pencil and paper and pens alike.

Impurities drained and blood let,

dried on stolen hotel robes and slippers,

wrapped in a plastic bag at the bottom of my closet.

I couldn't differentiate the deep end, so I sank all the way.


For I haven't felt a holiday in years, even with the resurgence
of red ribbons and foot-deep snow.

Long-lost memories on a boat out to sea.

For how gouged and scored deep down I had made it.

Maybe there are some things greater or better, but at least I found something of me.

For lately, my poetry is bad.

I have nothing to write about except real tragedy.

I'm fine, however.

I honestly haven't felt anything since my dose went up.

Just as potent: the loathing I feel for those who forget that from war comes death and grief, not pride.

Truthfully, I'm exhausted. I want to go home, and I'm already here.

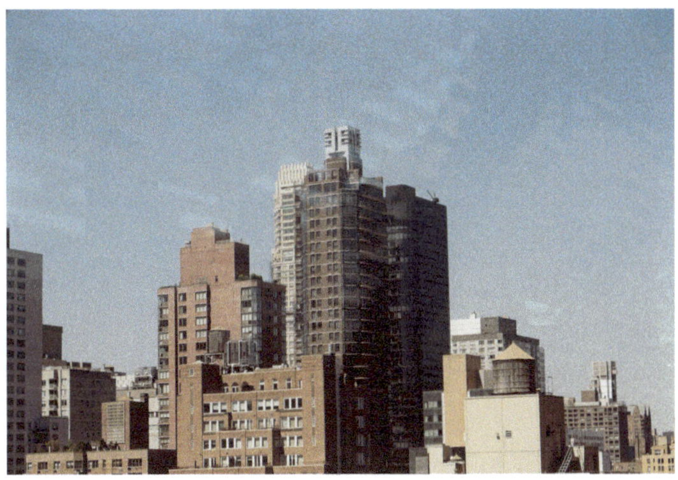

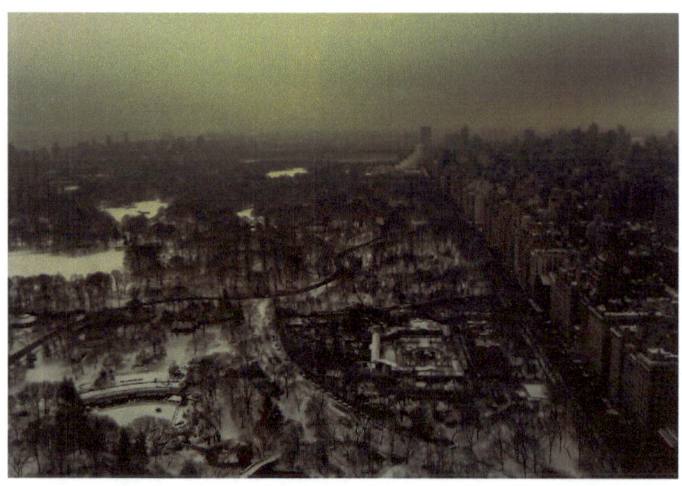

It's all about self-care until you owe everyone your opinion.

Ice skating at 33 degrees. Dissociating from human tragedy would just be easier.

My generation's hobby, the commodity to disconnect, unplug, and distance from everyone else's worse problems.

We've never been more connected.

And yet, I'm lonely.

I don't know who my friends are in this silent sardine-tin room.

I suppose some ornate facts impress my family. My scores satisfy my school. And silence appeases my friends.

When my left brain and my right brain lack the nerve to talk amongst themselves, I've lost myself. I've lost readers. The people who laugh at screens of my cumulative vulnerabilities.

I think of all the beautiful things I have seen.

Things that have glistened a hundred times over—

like the rainy pavement drying in the sun as I pull into my driveway, "closing doors I don't even know I am closing" yet.

I am a million full, college-ruled notebooks that weren't memorized for the test.

It's all hazy at the bottom of the mid-spring trash can.

There have easily been a million opportunities for an Upper East Side boy like me,

oblivious and slightly obnoxious with the whole world at my fingertips and business-casual concrete underneath my worn-out sneakers.

Every street lamp in front of me was some kind of star extinguishing itself,

its very last lingering flames.

And so I make another metaphor about how apparently I'm "burning out."

Yet, I think of the passionate stars

and I feel just a little bit better.

I could say that I've grown. I'm a different person now. Look! I've got a photo from "a year ago today" to prove it!

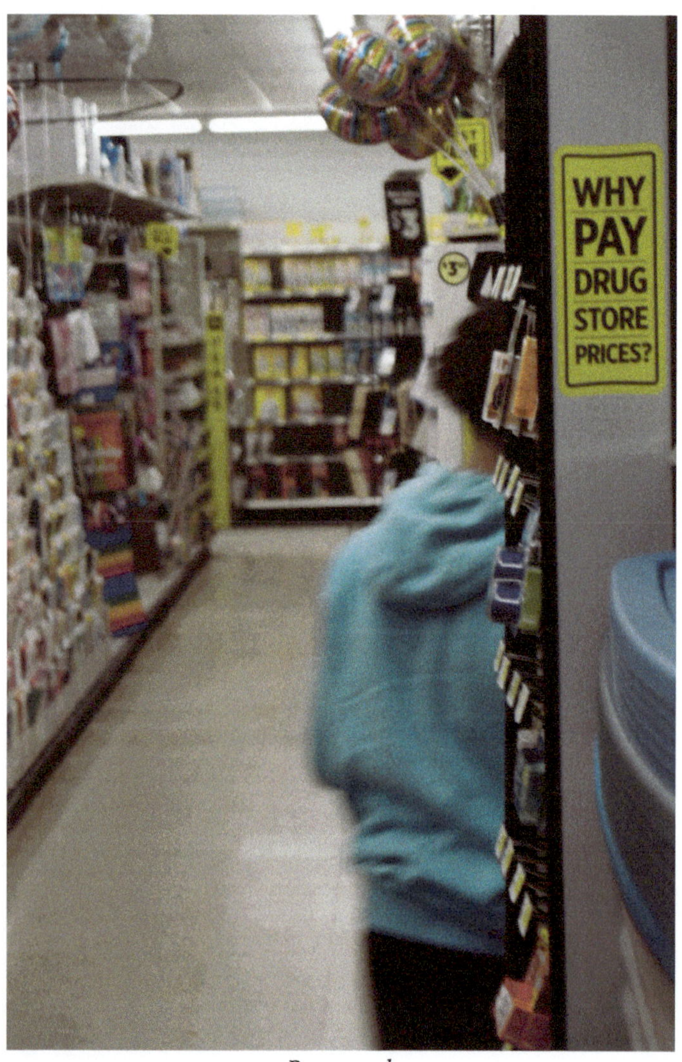


*Buzzwords*

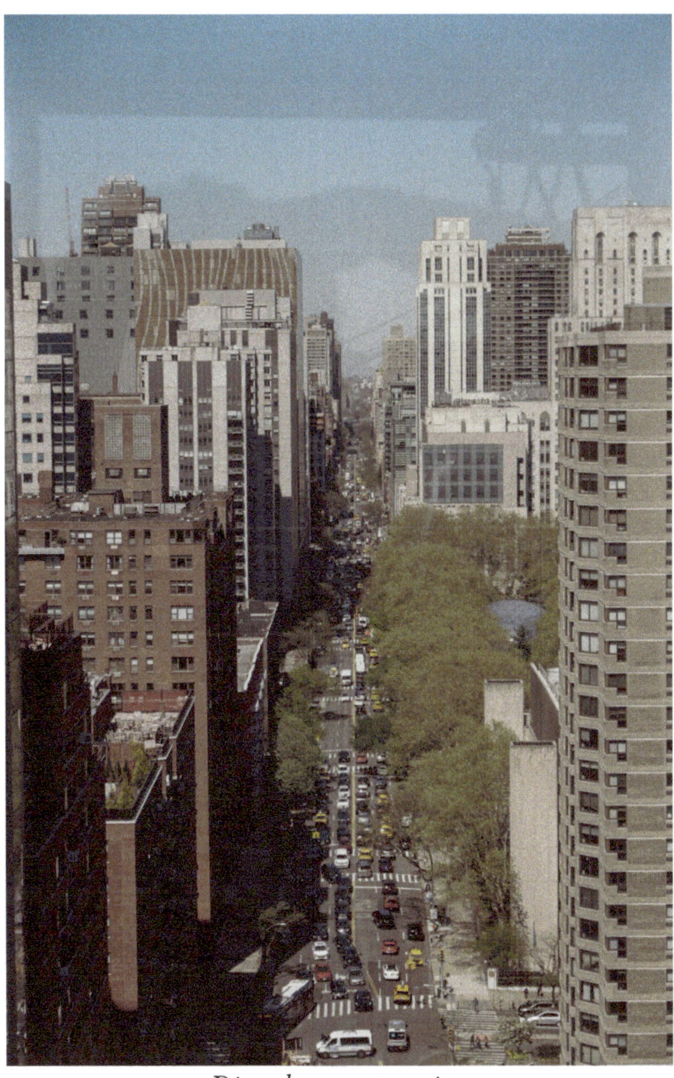

*Discord among promises.*

# ACT III
## CATASTROPHE

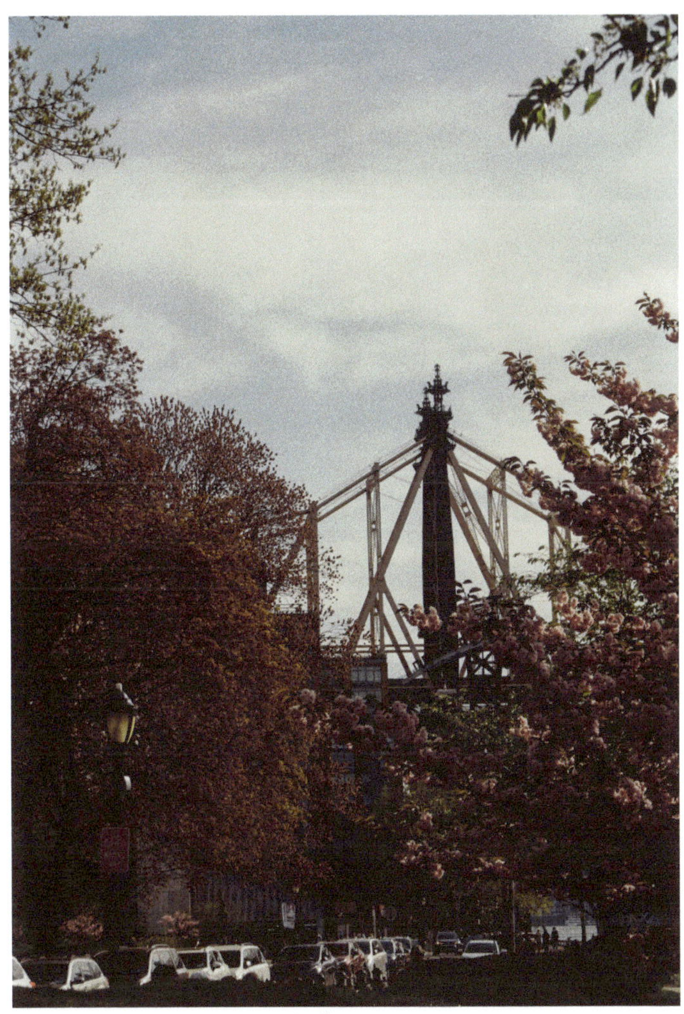

*Reframing*

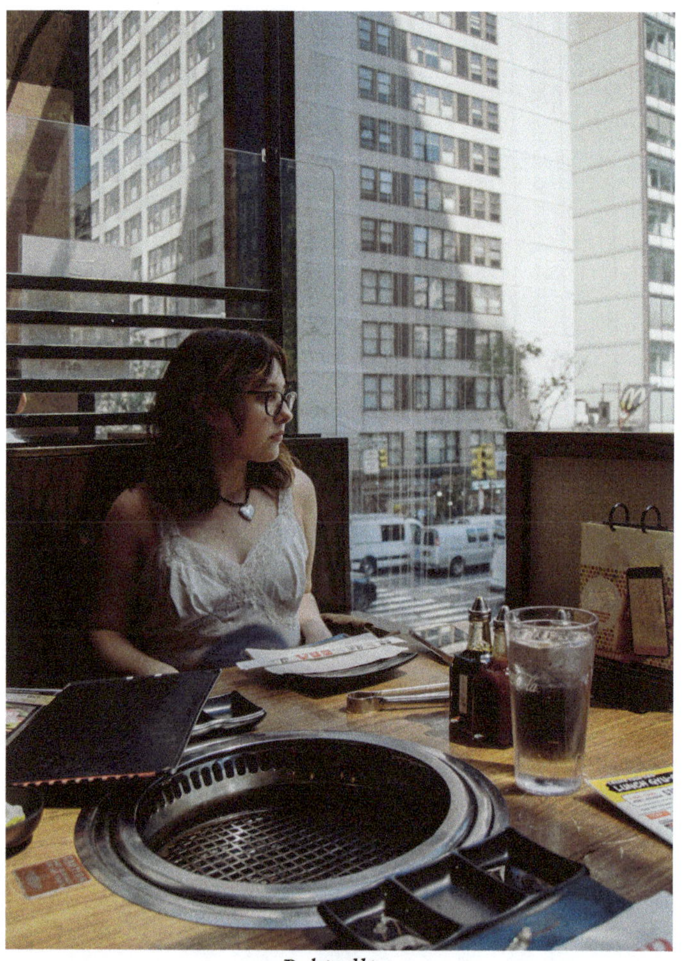

*Rekindling*

We made an assumption that the grass stayed right where it was.

Even after nightfall, through the next day or so—stagnant and eternal.


Eternal, like the memory of us dancing.
Sweat on our brows and my seventies button-down.


The search, the aid for your ail, the right path:
I've heard of mindfulness, or philosophy, or waiting in line at the pharmacy.


In your search for eternity, the fruit fly has found a new, more inspiring muse while I've done some thinking about the antonym of a warm embrace.

Perhaps it is that flinch at a light touch—the crumpling of butterfly wings.

Or, it's the shattering of a dozen raindrops on manicured lawns or indestructible vinyl tarps.

Of all the things I felt with you, slipping from your literal grasp and falling back into a tranquil field of clovers was the most wonderful.


Your weight—your baggage—was something I should've never carried alone.

When you fall with me, bring your day-bag with a good book and a bottle of ice water, for the post-impressionist painting of us has an empty patch of flowers for you, next to me.

When you fall with me, I'll take so many photos of us you will be disgusted by your camera for weeks on end.

When you fall with me, and I tell you I wrote a poem about us, don't ask me to read it aloud to you.

And finally, when you fall with me, don't ask me why.


Because the truth isn't something I can bear to materialize in this cruel world.

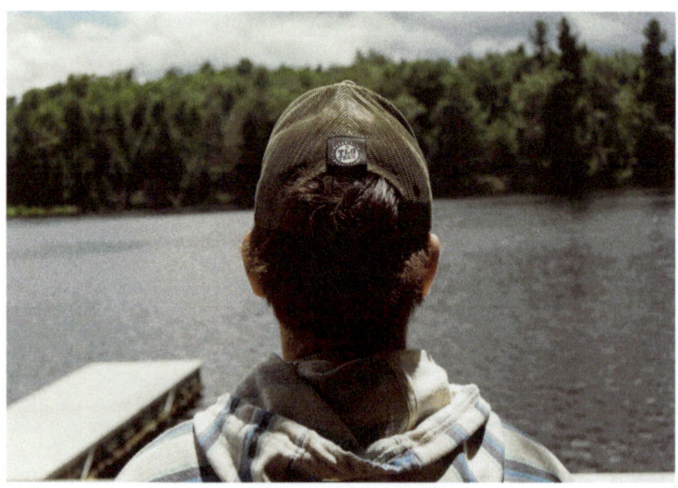

*Loyalty is a vow, a promise, a pact.*

Your new boy will ask you what your favorite color is.

Honestly, I hope you feel just a bit of pain in knowing that no one knows you like I do.

I know that your favorite color is green.

I know the numerous animal facts you relay to me.

I know what you know.

In that you know Santa Monica—

its pier and the forty-minute Sunday traffic to LAX.

It's why you leave soundlessly in the night, like a sheet swishing on a rooftop clothesline.

It cleans better in the moonlight than with that detergent you use.

I can't get the smell of your shirt, your detergent, off of me.

The hugs that could've put me to sleep are something I hide from.

You're like a metaphor in a spider web.

Venice, Charlie, Marina to Playa del Rey. Where you're at wealth's doorstep—

how real can you feel in a plastic factory?

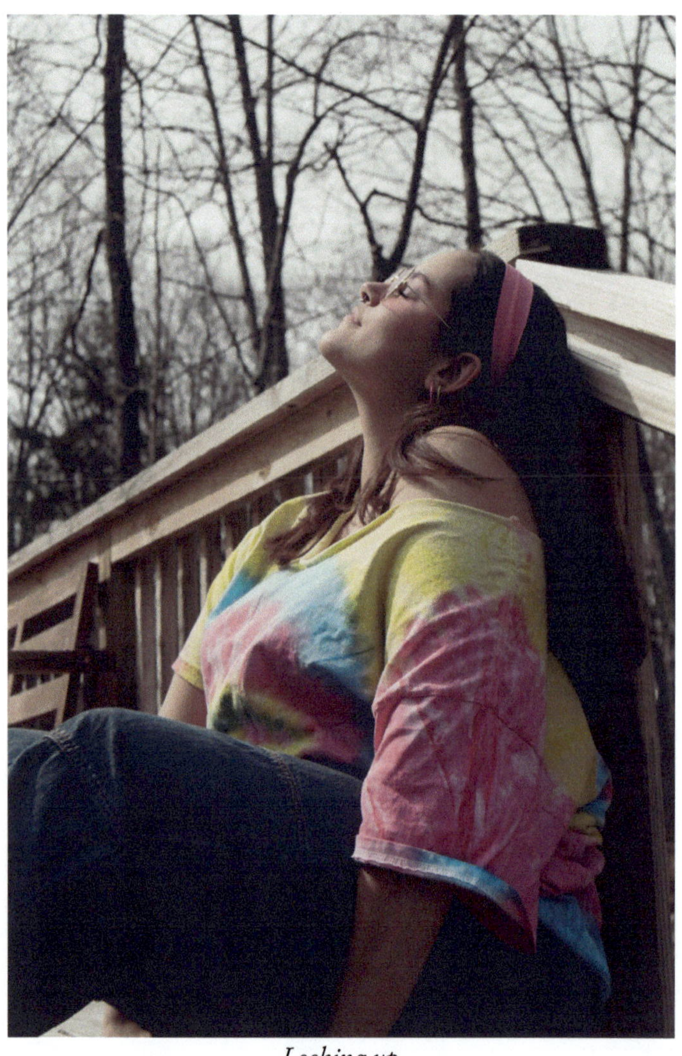

*Looking up.*

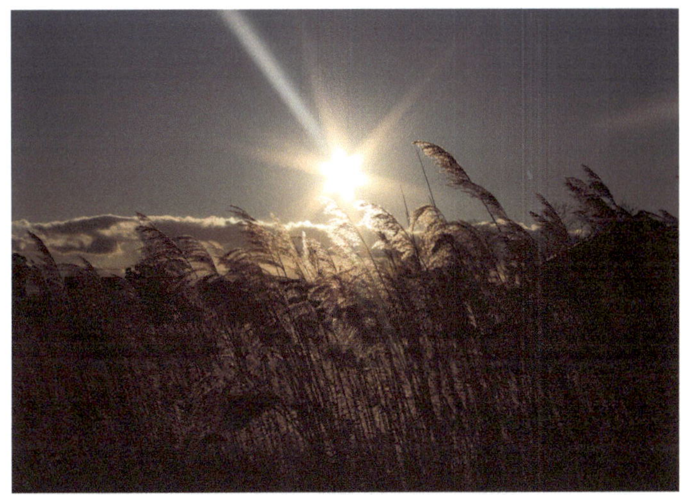

*I am free from the unraveling.*

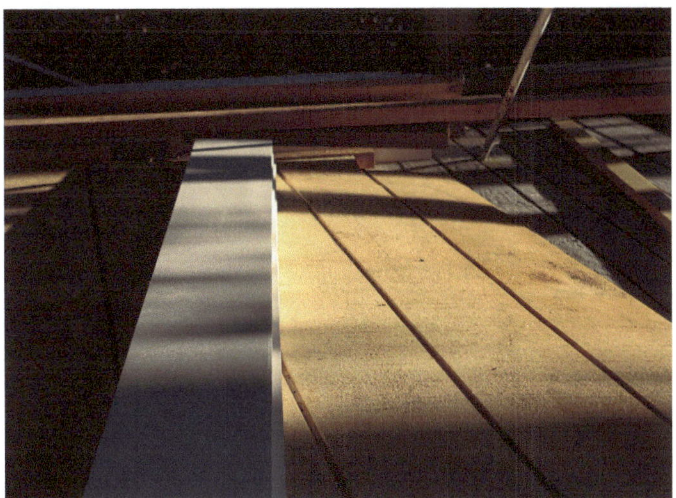

*Putting an end to sore fingertips. Death by stringing instruments.*

My rhetorical devices don't require answers.

I do return, however, to your misguided yearning for a world that never changes.

In stagnation, tranquility, and joy.

And I don't think that this "one right way" for this kind of eternity exists.

For there is no right without a left.

No love without hate.

No truth without dishonesty.

No loyalty without betrayal.

And for me,

my eternity, my answer, my path,

lies in the words on the page.

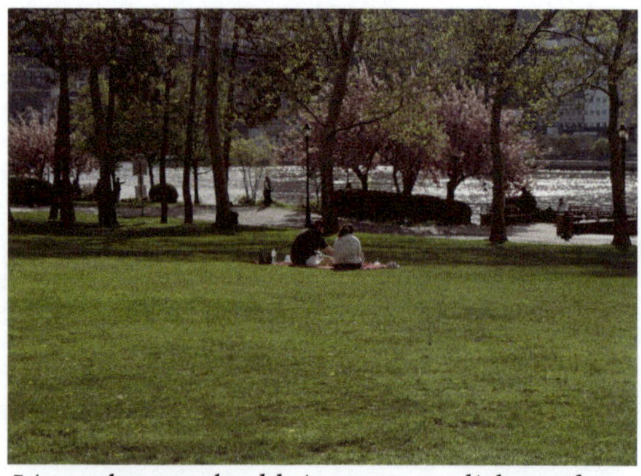

*It's not that you shouldn't question god's benevolence,*
*it's that you will live a miserable life doing so.*

# GALLERY

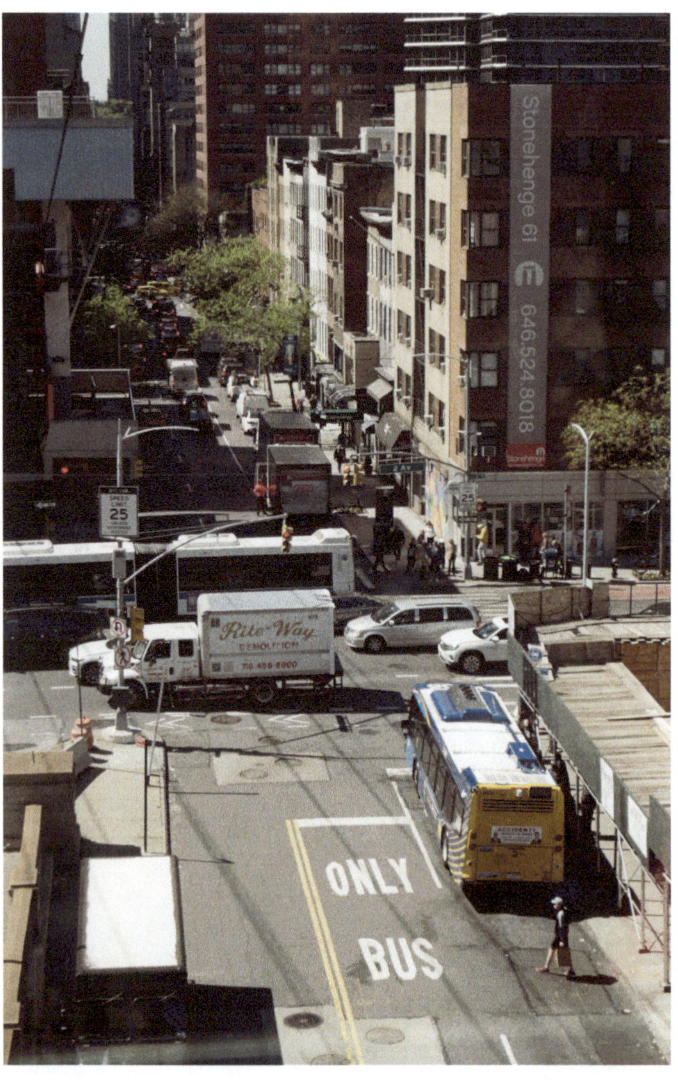
Stonehenge 61
646.524.8018
SPEED LIMIT 25
Rite Way
DEMOLITION
718 456-6900
ONLY
BUS

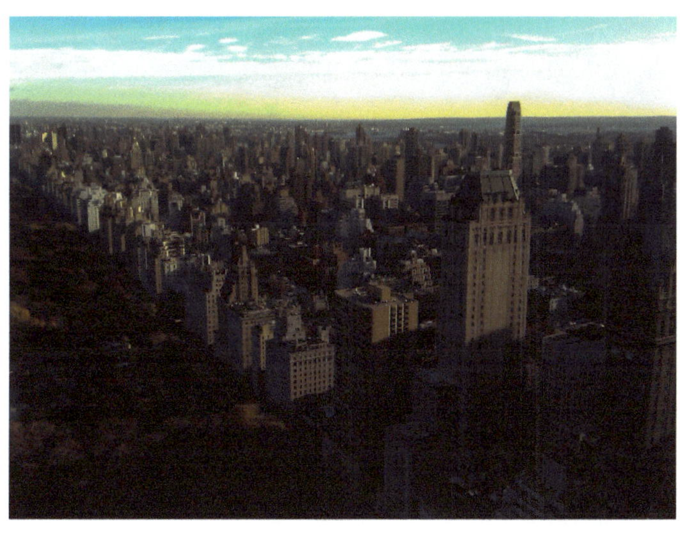

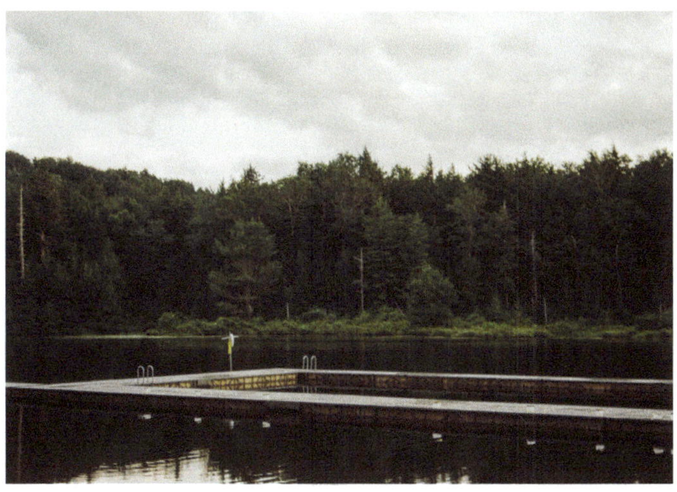

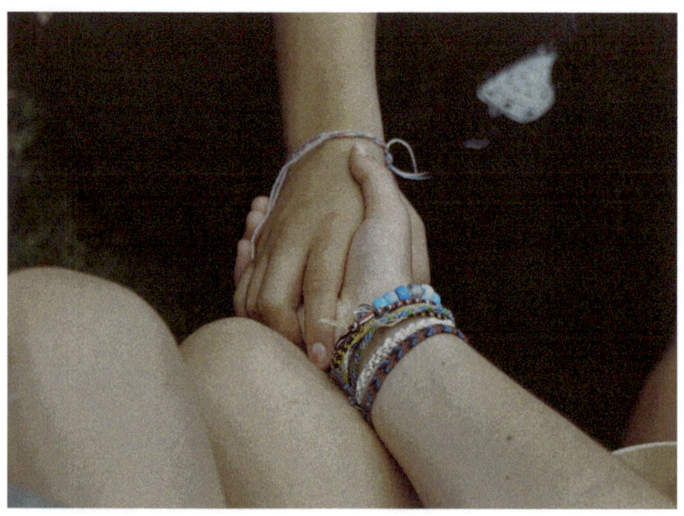

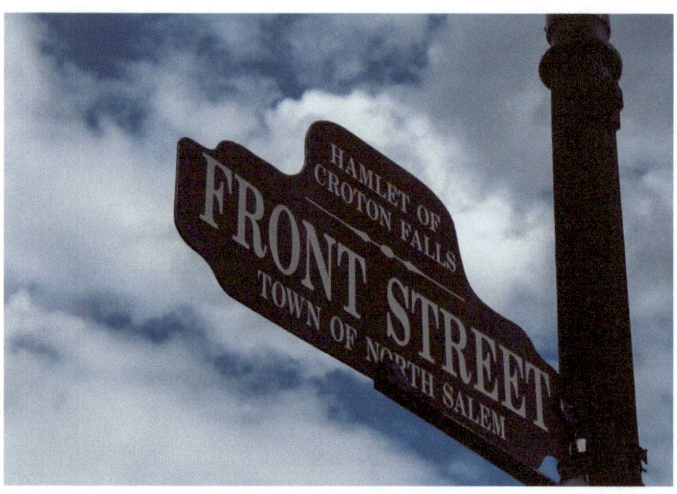
HAMLET OF
CROTON FALLS
FRONT STREET
TOWN OF NORTH SALEM

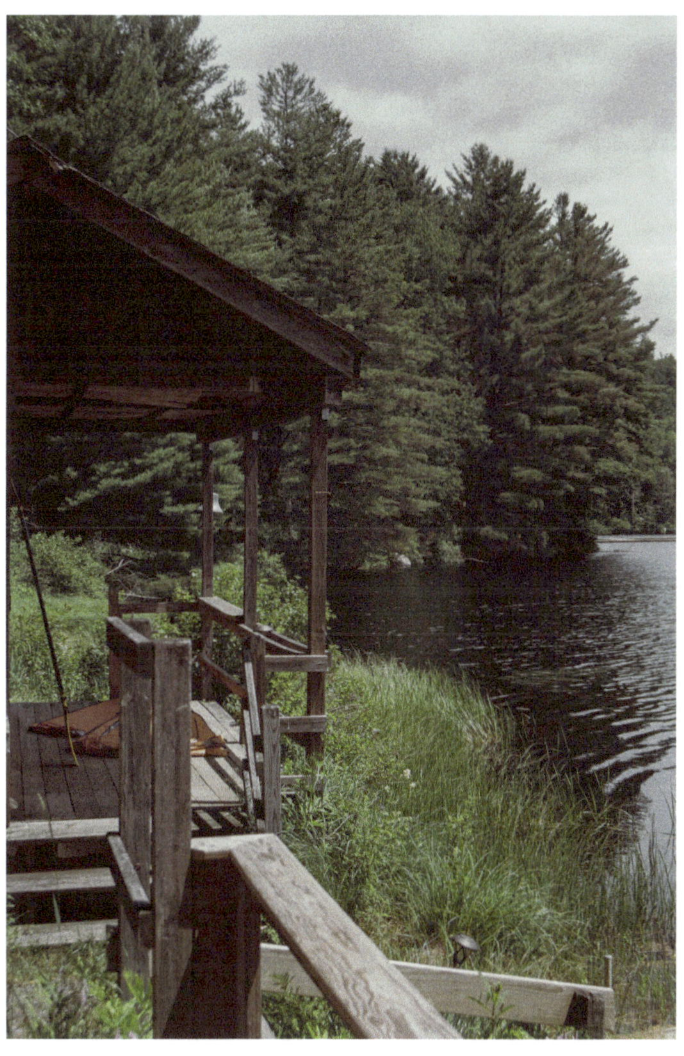

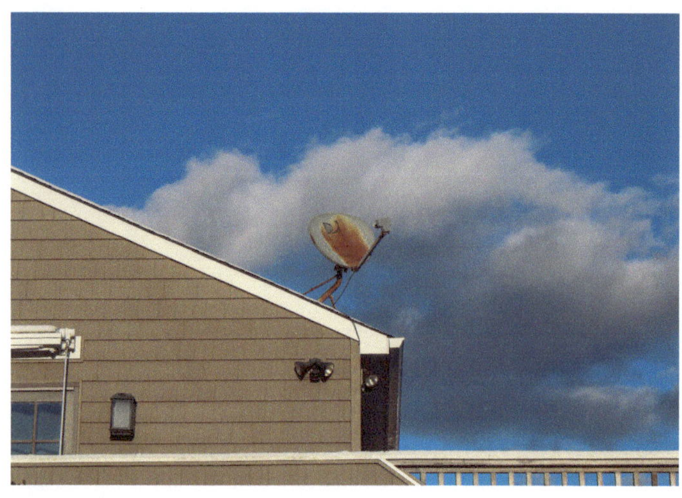

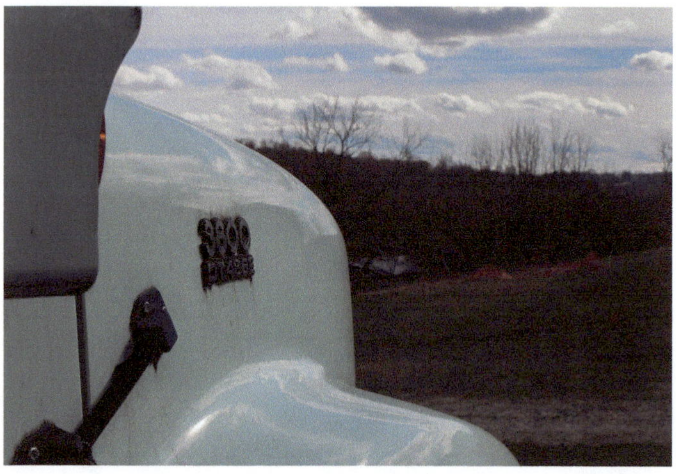

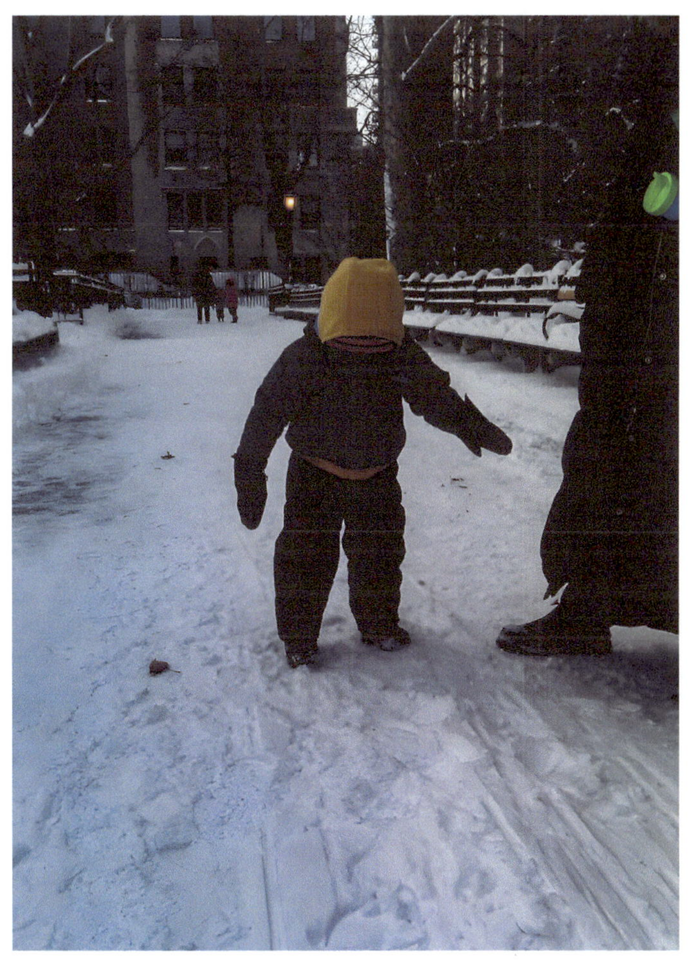

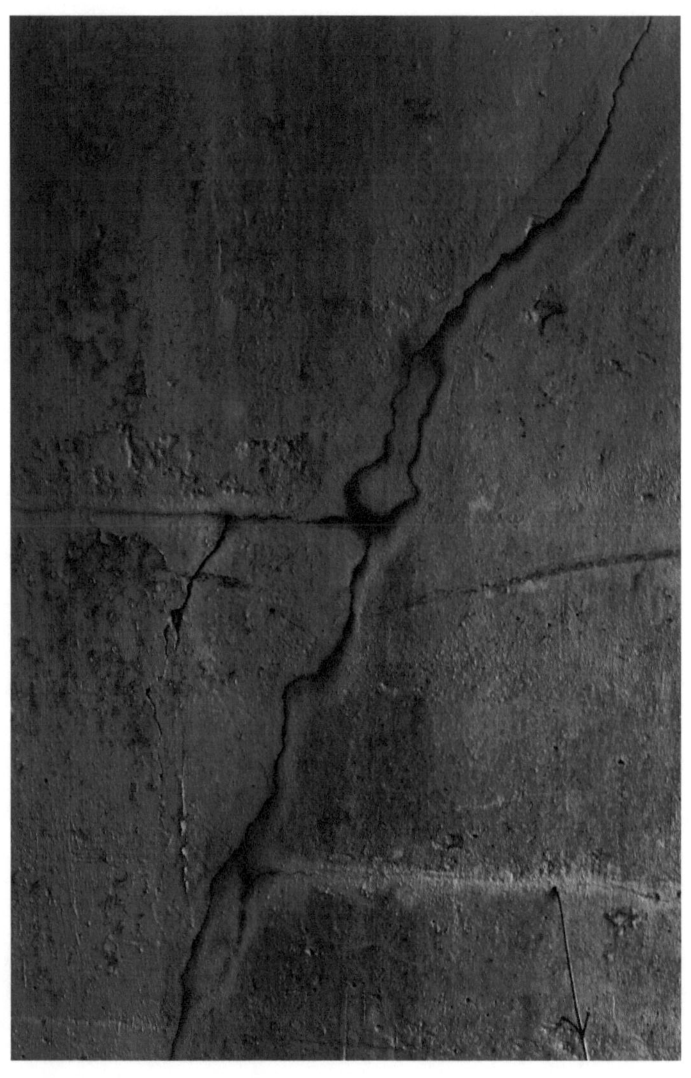

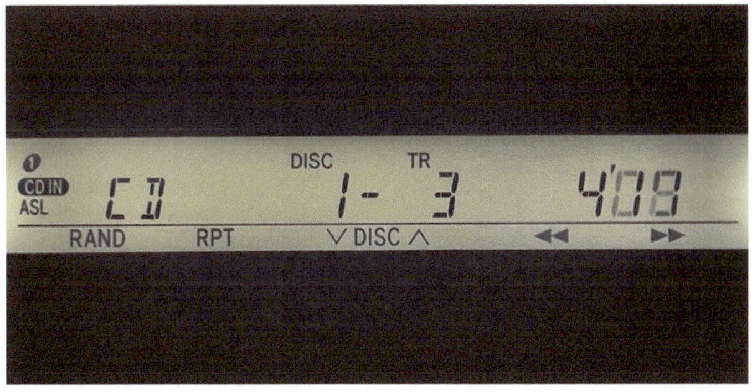

CD IN
ASL
CD
DISC
TR
1- 3
4'08
RAND
RPT
DISC


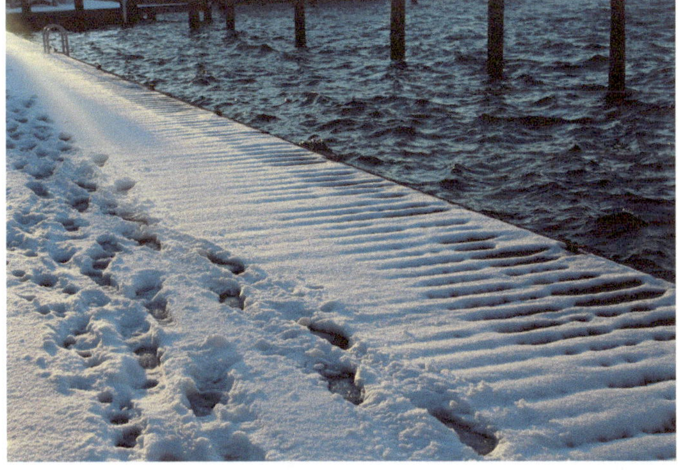

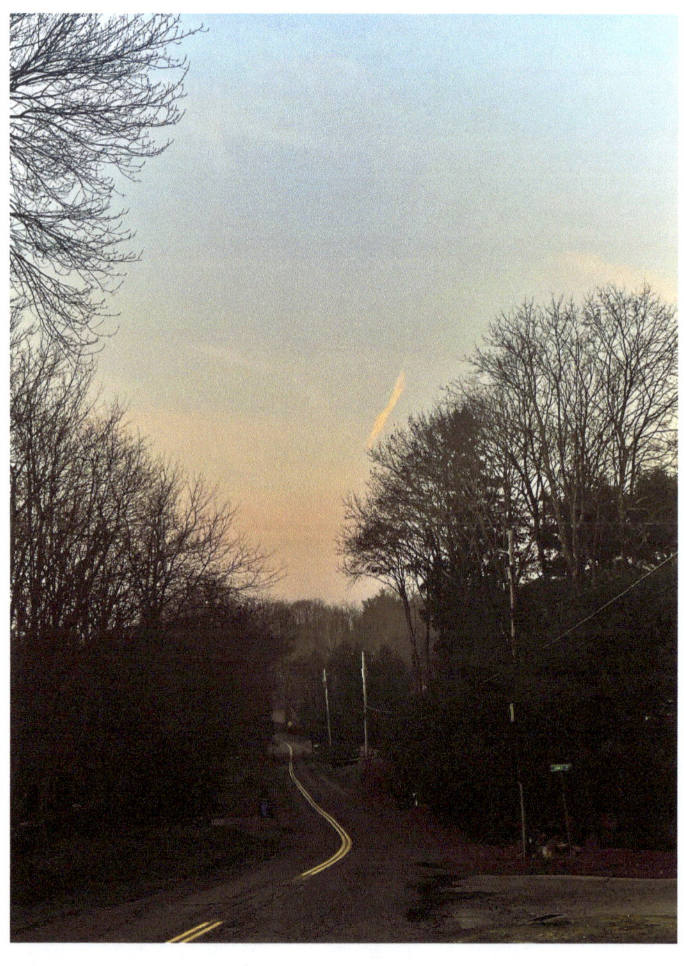

SEBASTIAN BERNINZONI was born and raised in New York City, later moving to Putnam County, NY. At the time of publishing, he is in 12th grade and studying at his local high school. Sebastian proudly announces *How the Muse Plays His Lyre* around a year after the release of his charting debut book *Us in the Flesh* in October of 2023. In addition to poetry and photography, he also spends his time petting his two cats, dabbling in the fiber arts, and drinking all the coffee he can get his hands on.

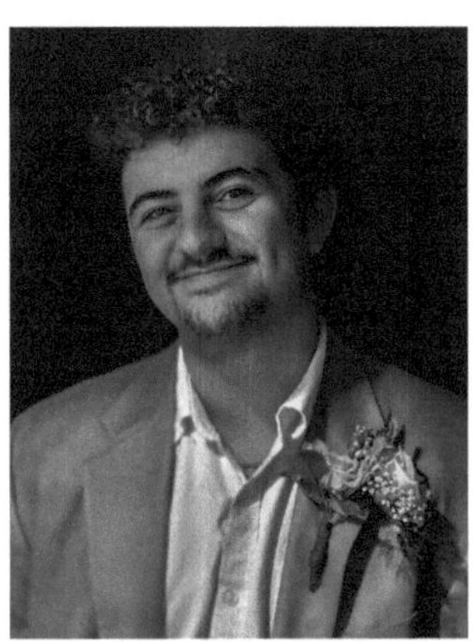

* 9 7 9 8 2 1 8 5 0 0 7 4 0 *